THE FAMOUS LION

RICHARD BRASSEY

Jonathan Cape
Thirty Bedford Square London

3954

There was once a famous lion . . .

In the town where he lived,
the people had put up
many fine statues of him
because he was so famous.

If you stood outside his house for long enough and were lucky, you might have caught a glimpse of him, coming in or going out.

But because he was so famous, he often used the back door.

One morning after breakfast,
the lion decided he was tired of
being famous. He came out on to
his balcony and told the people
who were waiting to see him,
"I am not famous any more,
so please go away."

He then told his servant to sell
his house and give away all his money
except enough for an aeroplane
ticket to an unknown destination.

Taking off his fine clothes,
he put on a rather ordinary grey
suit, and on his feet he wore
a pair of plimsolls.

He further changed his appearance
by shaving off his moustache.

When evening came, the famous lion
packed an overnight bag
with a few essentials . . .
a toothbrush, two clean pairs of
underpants and a large comb.
And pressing a flat cap firmly on
his head, he slipped out of
the back door into the darkness.

On his way to the airport,
he tripped over a small girl
who had lost a penny down a drain.
The famous lion hurt his knee.

This made him very late for
his aeroplane. When he arrived at
the airport, he went straight
to the controller and said, "I am
the famous lion. Stop the plane."
But, because he was wearing
a cloth cap and no moustache,
the controller replied,
"I don't believe you. For all I know,
you might be Higgeldy Pog,
the famous flying dog . . . although
you are a bit big for a dog."
And he laughed, "Ha! Ha!"
"I am not a dog," said the lion.
"I am travelling incognito."
"It's too late," said the controller.
"You've missed the plane."

The famous lion left the airport.
He decided to find a hotel
for the night and think what to do
next day. Remembering that he
no longer wished to be famous,
he told the man behind the desk at
the hotel, "My name is plain Mr Lion.
I am not at all well known."
So he was given a small room
on the top floor with only
a skylight and no window.
The famous lion slept badly.
In the morning his egg was hard.

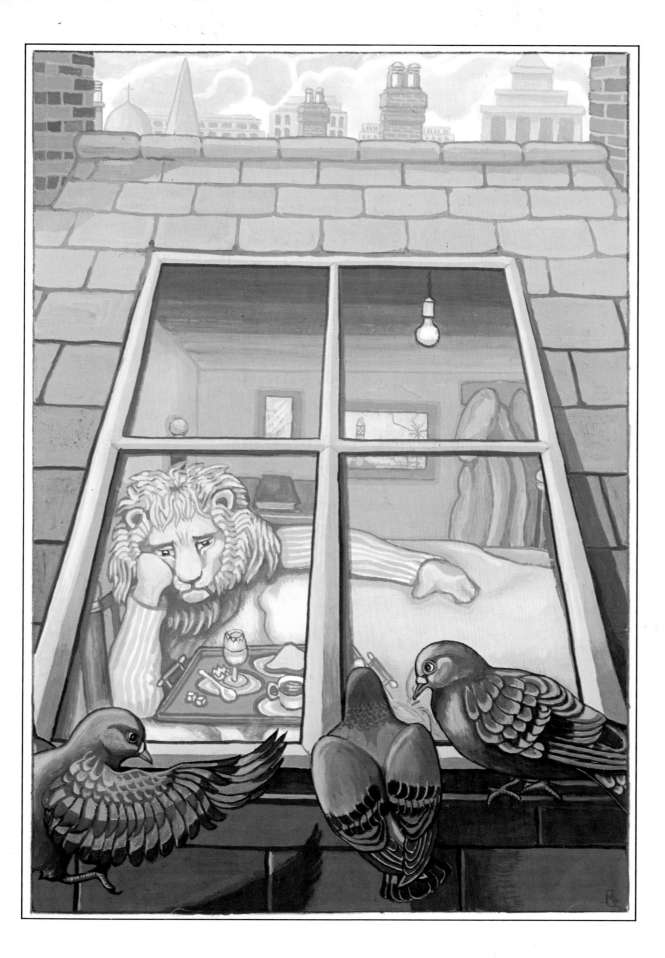

When the man at the hotel desk asked him to pay the bill, the lion remembered that he had no money.
"I am the famous lion," he said.
"I will send you the money
as soon as I can."
But the man did not believe him.
"If you cannot pay the
bill you will have to work in
the kitchen until you
have earned the money," he said.

The kitchen was hot and steamy.
The lion had to dry plates.
Because he had never dried plates before,
he was not very good at it
and kept dropping them on the floor.
The cook was not happy about this
and threw the lion out of the back door.

All the next night
the lion wandered up and down.
He had given away
his house and his money.
People no longer recognised him
and he was hungry.

In the morning he found a job
but he was no good at it.
He tried many jobs.
As autumn changed to winter
he grew thinner and thinner.
He tried heaving coal.
The sacks were very weighty
and they made his grey suit black.
It turned to rags.

Because he was tired and hungry,
he often fell over his own feet
and spilt the coal.
The coal merchant sent him away
with no money.

As he wandered along,
he met a small girl
who was selling matches.
"Do you think I could sell matches?"
he asked her.
"If I can," she replied,
"then a whopping great lion like you
should be able to."

The first day the lion tried
to sell matches, it rained
and they were ruined.
When the man who owned the matches
found out he took back the box
and kicked the lion over.

The lion was wet and tired and
hungry. He dragged himself under
the arches of a bridge
for shelter and fell into an
exhausted sleep. He was really down.

In the morning a smart man
nearly tripped over him.
"You are a lion, aren't you?"
he asked the famous lion.
The famous lion, who had been
dreaming of other things,
blinked and replied,
"Indeed, and not just any lion.
Famous is the word
you are searching for.
The famous lion at your service."
"And I . . ." said the smart man,
". . . am Napoleon Bonaparte,"
and he added that he supposed
the lion was the best he could find
at such short notice.

The smart man turned out to be
the ringmaster of a circus.
He dressed the lion
in an unusual costume
and taught him to do a daring act
using chairs and a hoop of fire.
The lion was not sure that
he enjoyed this, but at least he was
warm and dry, and Mr Bonaparte
gave him plenty to eat.

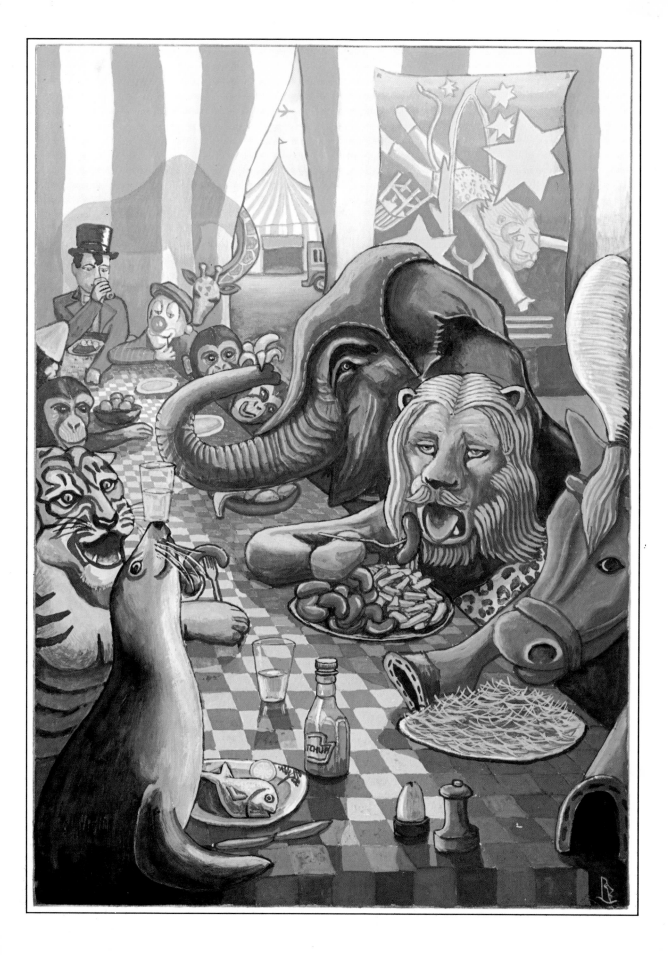

The circus travelled to
many parts of the world.
The lion learnt to do
new and surprising tricks.
People came from far and wide
to see him. When he made mistakes,
they only cheered louder.

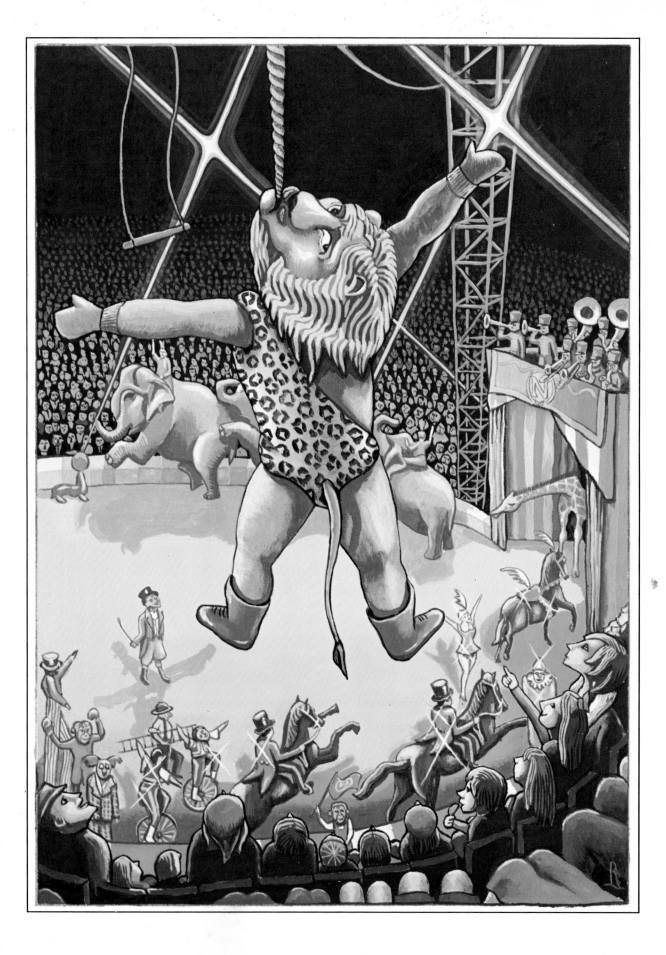

Nobles, princes and princesses
came to the circus—even kings
and queens. The King of Roartonia
thought the lion so good that
he made him "Sir" Lion
and gave him
a fairly large castle to live in.

The lion held hunting parties
there, to which many famous people
were invited. They ate
vast amounts of food
and strolled in the garden.

But the lion grew tired of company.
He now spends most of his time
in a magnificent town house,
which he bought with the money
he earned in the circus.
Even if you waited outside,
you would be very lucky to see him.

He seldom gets up before 12 o'clock
and hardly ever goes out.
But you can see
the statues of him
which the people of this town
have put up . . .

because he is so famous!

This book was written and illustrated
for Pikka who said,
"Tell me a story about
a famous lion."

First published 1980
© 1980 by Richard Brassey
Jonathan Cape Ltd, 30 Bedford Square, London WC1

British Library Cataloguing in Publication Data

Brassey, Richard
The famous lion.
I. Title
823'.9'1J   PZ7.B/
ISBN 0-224-01688-1

Printed in Great Britain by W S Cowell Ltd, Buttermarket, Ipswich